CURLFRIENDS
NEW IN TOWN

CHAPTER 14

CURLFRIENDS
NEW IN TOWN

SOLD

SHAREE MILLER

Coloring by Luke Healy

LB
INK

LITTLE, BROWN AND COMPANY
New York Boston

To my dad and my sister Adrienne

About This Book

The illustrations for this book were created by sketching in pencil, inking in Procreate, and coloring in Photoshop. This book was edited by Andrea Colvin and Nikki Garcia and designed by Jenny Kimura. The production was supervised by Bernadette Flinn, and the production editor was Marisa Finkelstein. The text was set in Sunbird Medium, and the display type was hand lettered by the artist.

Little, Brown Ink
Hachette Book Group
1290 Avenue of the Americas, New York, NY 10104
Visit us at LBYR.com

First Edition: October 2023

Little, Brown Ink is an imprint of Little, Brown and Company. The Little, Brown Ink name and logo are trademarks of Hachette Book Group, Inc.

The publisher is not responsible for websites (or their content) that are not owned by the publisher.

Little, Brown and Company books may be purchased in bulk for business, educational, or promotional use. For information, please contact your local bookseller or the Hachette Book Group Special Markets Department at special.markets@hbgusa.com.

Library of Congress Cataloging-in-Publication Data
Names: Miller, Sharee (Illustrator) | Title: Curlfriends : new in town / Sharee Miller. | Description: First edition. | New York : Little, Brown and Company, 2023. | Series: Curlfriends ; 1 | Audience: Ages 8–12. | Summary: Eager to make a good first impression at her new middle school, thirteen-year-old Charlie does her best to fit in until she meets a group of diverse Black girls who show her the importance of authenticity. | Identifiers: LCCN 2022060940 | ISBN 9780316591454 (trade paperback) | ISBN 9780316591478 (hardcover) | ISBN 9780316591447 (ebook) | Subjects: CYAC: Graphic novels. | Individuality—Fiction. | Middle schools—Fiction. | Schools—Fiction. | Friendship—Fiction. | African Americans—Fiction. | LCGFT: Graphic novels. | Classification: LCC PZ7.7.M553 Cu 2023 | DDC 741.5/973—dc23/eng/20221221 | LC record available at https://lccn.loc.gov/2022060940

ISBNs: 978-0-316-59147-8 (hardcover), 978-0-316-59145-4 (paperback), 978-0-316-59144-7 (ebook), 978-0-316-59326-7 (ebook), 978-0-316-59328-1 (ebook)

PRINTED IN CHINA

1010

Hardcover: 10 9 8 7 6 5 4 3 2 1
Paperback: 10 9 8 7 6 5 4 3 2 1

CHAPTER
1

If you could be anyone in the world, who would you be? An athlete? A nerd? How about the most popular girl in school? My name is Charlie Harper. I'm 12 years old and today is my first day of middle school.

I've had more first days than I can count. My dad's been in the US Air Force since I was born, which means we moved around a lot.

Every time we did, it meant a new school, new kids, and a new chance to make friends. That part has never been easy for me, especially when I transfer in three weeks late!

But not this time. I plan to completely reinvent myself, starting with my look.

I spent all summer reading fashion magazines and taking every friendship quiz I could.

I've never studied this much in my life, but all my preparation is about to pay off. My mom always says you only get one chance at a first impression, so today must go perfect.

Well, I think you look perfect. How about I make you some pancakes?

I already have cereal. Thanks.

Suit yourself. Morning, sweetheart.

Morning, hun.

VRRRR

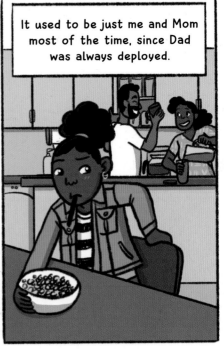

It used to be just me and Mom most of the time, since Dad was always deployed.

As for Mom, she's starting today as a pediatrician at Saint Katharine Hospital. She hasn't been back to work full-time since she had me. A lot of things are changing so fast.

It feels like my parents already have a place where they fit here. I'm just playing catch-up. I don't want to be left behind.

14

CHAPTER 2

SLIP

AHHH!

OWWW

HA HA HA HA

No, no, no. Why is this happening?!

Is she OK?

Wow, that was a hard fall.

25

Hey, are you OK?

AHH!

Sorry, sorry, I didn't mean to scare you. I'm Nola. I saw what happened out there. Do you need some help?

No, I'm fine, thanks. Unless you have a comb or a miracle.

Actually, you're in luck. I have both!

We're going out the window?!

Yeah, it's no big deal. Come on!

33

CHAPTER 3

I was able to make it through class without any more embarrassing incidents, even though no one got to see my awesome outfit, but now it's the worst part of the day.

Lunchtime is when people want to sit with their friends, not some random new girl. Should I just sit by myself?

No, I'll look like a loner, but if I sit at the wrong table, I might be stuck with people I don't like all year. Maybe I should go hide in the library.

No, if I hide, I won't make any friends. All right. Here goes nothing.

Hey, Nola!

Huh?

Oh, hey, it's you. Nice to see you again. I'm sorry, but I don't think I got your name.

Oh, it's Charlie. Um...can I eat with you?

Really? Why?

My dad was in the air force, so we moved around a lot, but he's retired now, so no more moving for me.

Wow. Where were you before here?

We just moved from London, actually.

Whoa, London? That's so cool! What's it like there?

It's pretty great. We were there for only a year, but my mom and I went to the Tate and rode on the London Eye. I even got to take one of those red double-decker buses to school every day.

So, Charlie, do you watch *Super Sailors?*

Huh? Oh, this sweatshirt? You know this show?

Yeah, I used to watch it when I was younger. I haven't seen it in years.

Oh yeah, me too. I just happened to grab it this morning.

Never heard of it.

It's a Korean cartoon.

Yeah, it's for babies, though.

49

Nope. Sorry, this was the only one they had. I keep telling you to come with me.

I just can't get into clothes that have already been worn. Yuck!

Careful, Nola, you know when Ella becomes president, she is going to outlaw fast fashion, right?

Fast fashion *IS* one of the leading causes of global warming!

53

Look on the bright side. At least no one recorded it. That would've been a billion times worse.

Good thing I was there. I saved the day with my quick braiding skills.

Shooo Shooo

I was wondering how you got your hair fixed so quickly. You're lucky--I would drop out of school if I had to walk around all day soaking wet with messed-up hair.

Chill, Ella. No one wants to keep talking about their most embarrassing moment.

CHAPTER 4

That's lovely, Charlie!

Thanks! Art is my favorite class.

I'm happy to hear that.

I can see from your technique that you practice a lot!

I do! Every chance I get. Mostly in my sketchbook. I don't usually share it.

That's too bad. You should share your art.

Yeah, Mr. Carter, right?

Yes, that's right. Please take your seats.

Oh, yes, a seat...

Charlie! Hey, Charlie, over here.

Now that everyone is seated, we can begin. Today we will be discussing our first group project.

What, already? It's only my first week. Man, I hate starting school late.

Both of you pay attention, please.

Sorry!

Sorry, Mr. Carter.

I want you to break out into groups of four. You have eight minutes. Please hurry.

GULP

Groups?

Hey, Charlie. Come be in our group!

OK.

Great, now we just need to know the topic and break up the work evenly. I had the best grades in science last year, so I'll be the team captain.

Did he say we need a team captain?

Doesn't matter. Ella is always in charge. It's easier if you just go with it.

I think the point of the project is to work together.

What? I just want everything to run smoothly.

Fine, just don't let it go to your head like last time.

What about you, Charlie?
Do you have any ideas?

Me?! Um...
I don't know. What
about you?

Ugh, no, I hate
science. I can't even
think of anything.

CHAPTER 5

Mom's still not here yet?

NO MESSAGES

I guess I'll sketch till she comes.

All their compliments did make me want to draw more.

82

We're home!

Head upstairs and start on your homework while I make dinner.

OK.

89

What do you think, Pierre?

Purrrfect? He-he.

Charlie, dinner's ready--

What's all this? This doesn't look like homework.

Huh? It is. It's, um, research for an art project.

Hm, exactly what kind of research are you doing with fashion magazines?

Well...we have to do a self-portrait. Yeah...and I was thinking of doing a collage.

I see. Just make sure you put as much effort into your other work, too. Not only art class. I know art is fun, but you also have to focus on your other subjects if you want to be successful.

Yeah, I know. I'm just excited about this project.

Coming.

Well, hurry down for dinner. Mom made your favorite, spaghetti and meatballs.

Huh? Oh, it was OK, I guess.

My art teacher is really nice.

Oh good! I'm excited to see what you make this year.

Thanks, Mom.

What about your classmates? Did you make any friends?

Well, I have a class project with some girls, and they seem nice. One of them is kind of bossy, though.

Well, maybe she won't seem so bossy once you get to know her better.

Maybe...

I remember my first day of middle school. Joey and I had everyone wrapped around our fingers by lunchtime. We shot free throws in gym, and the coach made us join the team on the spot.

On your first day?

Yep. They called me Hoops for the rest of the year.

Don't you have gym tomorrow? Make sure you pack your gym clothes.

Ugh don't remind me.

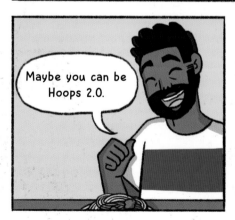

Maybe you can be Hoops 2.0.

No way. You know I'm not good at sports.

CHAPTER 6

Charlie, what's taking so long?

KNOCK KNOCK KNOCK

Mom, help.

Whoa. Put the flat iron down. Come out here and let me see what I can do.

Why didn't you just leave the braids in? They were so cute.

PLOP

Sure, they were fine in a pinch, but they didn't go with the look.

Made it!

Now I just have to get to class without any surprises.

Hey, Charlie.

Wanna walk to class together?

AHH!

Nola?! You startled me!

It's called Carol's Curls after my grandma Carol. All our customers give us five stars!

Cool. I can't wait to check it out.

Well, here we are. Taking the long way is fun sometimes. It gives you time to chat.

You're right. I didn't even notice we were here.

I'll see you at lunch.

Yeah, see ya.

No way. I had bacon, eggs, pancakes, and hot tea just like I do every morning, but I ran it all away during my morning jog.

Wow, you work out a lot, don't you?

Yep, and I have track practice after school, too.

No wonder you're so hungry all the time.

Gotta keep fueled up!

You OK, Charlie?

Yeah. ⇒*wheeze*⇐ I just... don't run much.

It's fine. It's not a race.

You don't...have to...run slow to... keep pace with me. Go on ahead.

Wow, I was really holding her back.

Hey, are you all right?

Y-yeah, I think so.

There you go. I'm Conn, by the way.

I'm--

Charlie!!!

Charlie! I'm so sorry. I saw you fall.

Are you hurt anywhere? Let me see!

I'm fine, just a little scratched up. Conn here helped me out.

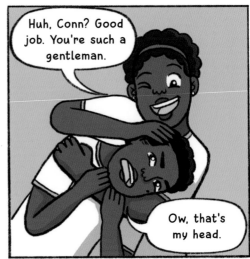

Huh, Conn? Good job. You're such a gentleman.

Ow, that's my head.

Oh, you two know each other?

Of course. Oh, I guess you don't know. This is my twin brother, Conn!

MERCY! MERCY!

Twin?!

Yep. Fraternal, obviously.

CHAPTER 7

126

Here, I added all our numbers to your phone. I even made us a group!

Curlfriends?

It's just our group nickname, since we're friends and we all have curly hair. Isn't it cute?

Yeah. Thanks for adding me.

No problem. It will make it easier to plan for the project.

For the project... right.

Oh, and you should thrift with us tomorrow.

And we're gonna grab boba after.

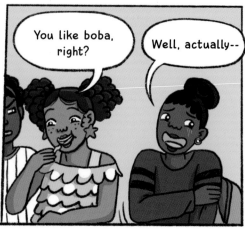

You like boba, right?

Well, actually--

You must come and let me make you an apology outfit for running my mouth yesterday!

An apology outfit?

Yeah, I make upcycled clothing from thrift store finds. Take anything with a fun pattern and I can whip you up something cool and totally "you" with my trusty sewing machine. This shirt was once a skirt.

Oh, that's cool, but--

Yep, you're not the only artist here.

I never said I was...

Hey, y'all. What did I miss?

Charlie is going thrifting with us tomorrow.

Awesome.

Wait. I mean, I still have to ask my parents.

Sure, sure. Just text us what they say.

By the way, it was bugging me all morning, but I finally realized where I saw your outfit.

In last month's *Teen Style* magazine.

I had it in my locker, and I remember thinking how cute that outfit was.

Lemme see!

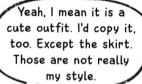

Yeah, I mean it is a cute outfit. I'd copy it, too. Except the skirt. Those are not really my style.

I'd rock it, but with a different top.

The shoes are my favorite. Where did you get those, Charlie?

Um, online somewhere. I don't really remember.

Doesn't it say where to get everything in the magazine?

RiiiiiNNNG

Today we'll be drawing from life. Still lifes are a great way to practice observation.

Being able to see things for how they are and not how we imagine them to be is a real skill.

SQUINT

Ugh. My contacts are getting so dry. It's hard to focus.

This is looking lovely so far.

Oh, thanks. It would be better, but my contacts are bothering me.

Oh no. Do you have eye drops or your glasses?

No, I forgot them.

Do you want to see if the nurse has any?

I'll be fine. The day is almost over.

OK, but let me know if it gets any worse.

Thanks, I will.

By the way, I love what you ended up doing for your self-portrait.

What made you think to use magazine clippings?

It just...came to me.

Well, I love it. Keep up the great work.

Yeah...

Hey guys, look at this website I found with info on butterflies.

Apparently, caterpillars make enzymes that completely digest their caterpillar bodies and then they rebuild themselves into a butterfly.

Whoa, that's gross. Tell me more.

EWWW!

So, it really is a complete transformation.

Don't worry. We still have time to get a lot done this weekend at Cara's house.

Oh yeah, if you bring all the supplies you need, we should be good.

Just make sure you keep your brothers out of the way, Cara.

CHAPTER
8

Ugh.

My eyes are killing me. Hopefully Mom comes soon.

Oh, she's on time today.

BEEP
BEEP

Mom, how was wor--

Dad?

Where's Mom?

She's still at work, so I get to pick you up.

Oh, she's always picked me up in the past.

You know your mom was part-time before. Now her schedule isn't as open, but I make my own hours, so I'll be picking you up from now on.

She didn't tell me that.

I wanted to surprise you. What's going on with your eyes? They're red.

It's fine. My eyes are just a little dry from the contacts.

What about your eye drops?

I forgot them at home.

Hey, how about we grab some cheese puffs?

Pfft, no way. Mom will have a fit. Don't you remember the frozen pizza disaster of 2015?

Oh yeah, almonds it is, then.

Mom always says that you're going to eat unhealthy things while you're out, but at home...

...we only eat real food.

HA HA HA

If we hurry, we can grab some ice cream on the way home.

Yes, please!

All we need now is cereal, and then it's ice-cream time.

So, how is school going? How many friends have you made so far?

You asked me that yesterday.

I know. I'm just excited for you. I met some of my best friends at that same middle school.

PAT PAT

Yeah, I know, Dad.

That's one of the reasons we moved back here. I--

Jacob? Jacob, is that you?

Hi.

Um, Dad, I'm gonna go grab the cereal.

OK, be right there. So, what have you been up to, man?

STOMP
STOMP
STOMP

It's not fair. At least everywhere else, we were all in the same boat. We only knew one another.

A salon? Why?

My classmate's mom owns it, and she said to stop by if I'm ever around.

Thanks. It's nice to meet one of Charlie's fri--

We were across the street, and I noticed the sign.

Oh yeah, the lights were my idea!

Hold on, let me get my mom.

Mama!

Chantel and I went to school together. We go way back.

Really? That's cool!

A lot of our classmates never really moved away, but Jacob here just had to see the world. What about you and Margo?

Married 20 years. You should come over for dinner sometime.

Sorry, I had no idea our parents knew each other.

Why are you sorry?

My dad just goes on and on whenever he sees someone he grew up with. Which seems to be everyone in town.

I think it's great. They're so happy to see each other. It's so cool to know someone that long.

Yeah, I guess.

HA HA HA HA HA

Why does he have to know everybody? He makes it seem so easy.

BUZZ BUZZ

Welcome to the text chain, Charlie!

 Yass! Now we can let you know about all the fun things to do in town!!!

 Can't wait to introduce you to the world of thrifting. Here's the address. Ask your parents so we can go right after school! TTYL

Could be fun...

What could be fun?

Dad?! Are you spying on me?

No, you were just talking to yourself with the door open. So, what's going on?

Nothing. Nola and some other girls at school just invited me to go thrift shopping with them tomorrow, but I don't think I'm going to go.

What? Why not?

The only reason they gave me their numbers was to talk about schoolwork. I don't want to be a pity invite.

No way. They wouldn't have invited you if they didn't want to hang out.

I guess, but they're also getting boba, and that stuff makes me gag.

Just get the tea without the boba. If you tell them it makes you sick, I'm sure they'll understand.

I'll let your mom know. Text when you're done, and one of us will pick you up. The only way to make friends is to put yourself out there.

I'll be there.

CHAPTER 9

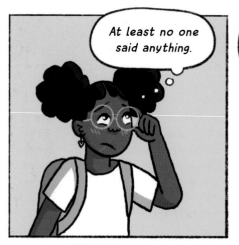

At least no one said anything.

Hopefully I can make it through thrifting with my secret weapon.

These clippings will help me stay on trend at the thrift store.

As long as no one notices, I'll be good.

Charlie! Have you been waiting long?

Get excited. This place even has designer clothes sometimes, since we are so close to New York City.

By that, she means she found a Marc Jacobs wallet once.

Yes, and guess who has a *Marc Jacobs* wallet for ten dollars? Me!

Anyway, Charlie, I heard you are an only child like me!

Yeah. That's right.

You two are so lucky. Being a responsible big sister is so much pressure.

Oh please, you love bossing your little brother and sister around.

It can be kind of lonely sometimes, though.

Yeah, but that's what friends are for, right?

TA DAH

These? I mean, sure, these are trendy, but they don't really feel like you.

PROUD

What do you mean?

What about those overalls? They were cute.

What? No way. Overalls are a big fashion no-no.

No way, says who? You just have to style them right.

I don't think so.

Thank you.

Careful, don't choke.

SLURP!

Ahh! But they're so good! The bubbles are my favorite part.

Yum

Charlie, you haven't touched yours. Is it OK?

Oh, yeah. I'm just savoring it. Mmm.

HEH HEH HEH

197

Feel better, Charlie.

Yeah, feel better.

Take it easy.

Thanks, you guys. See you tomorrow.

SIGH

SLIDE

Do you want to tell me what's going on, young lady?

CHAPTER
10

Ha-ha, yeah. So, do you wanna walk to class together?

Actually, I have to run and return a book to the library before class. Sorry.

Bye, Charlie. Glad you're feeling better.

Thanks! I'll see you later...

Oh no. Ella, what about your house?

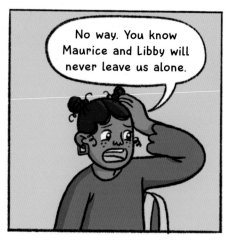

No way. You know Maurice and Libby will never leave us alone.

I guess we can do it at my apartment, but it will be a tight squeeze.

We can do it at my house!

Really? That would be great.

Of course! Why didn't I think of that?

Are you sure it's fine?

Of course. I'll tell my parents it moved from Cara's house to ours. We have plenty of room, and it's quiet.

Your house is so big and beautiful. I'm sure your room is huge.

As long as it's cleaner than Cara's messy room, I'm happy.

Hey! I like to think of it as organized chaos.

My room!

GULP

Where am I gonna put all this stuff before tomorrow?

Is everything OK, Charlie?

Yeah, just cleaning up for our project session tomorrow.

Good idea. This place is a mess. I'm going to run out and get some fruit for your friends. Any special requests?

I'm sure whatever you get will be fine, Mom.

Ooh, I wonder if the store has any mangoes.

Snacks are the least of my problem.

I just have to get all this embarrassing stuff out of here.

CHAPTER
11

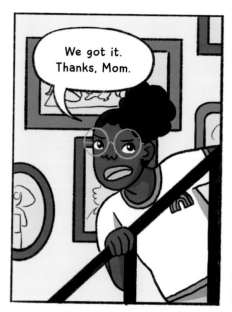

We got it.
Thanks, Mom.

Yell if you
need anything.

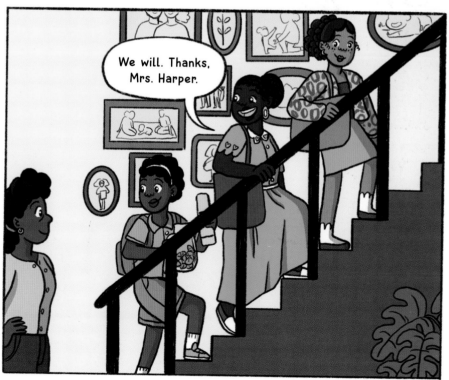

We will. Thanks,
Mrs. Harper.

Where's all your stuff?

Um, I like very minimal decor.

Oh, that's cool. I guess.

Whoa, I thought that was a stuffed animal.

STRETCH

MEOW

No, that's just Pierre, my cat. He's really lazy. No stuffed animals here.

PURRRR

Oh yeah. Maybe I should open it later, though. We have a lot of work to do.

Yeah. Totally. It can wait.

Thanks.

This is the poster paper for the final presentation.

Do you think we have enough to fill it?

Yeah! I sketched up some ideas last night. Check it out.

This will be so awesome on Monday.

Yeah. It turned out really beautiful, thanks to Charlie's skills.

You all helped a lot with the coloring, too.

Now that we're done, you have to open your gift. I want to see your face when you see it.

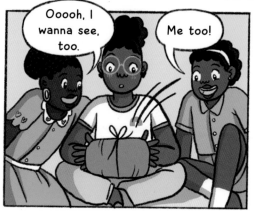

Ooooh, I wanna see, too.

Me too!

Sure. Let me open it.

Wow, those are so cute.

Yeah, great job, Ella.

...Yeah, great job.

I know you said you didn't like them, but I knew if you saw them after I worked my magic you would change your mind.

Everything OK, Charlie?

Yeah, I'm just...hungry! I'm gonna go get us some more snacks. I'll be right back.

TOSS

She would if she gave them a chance.

Don't you think they're cute?

Well, yeah, but...

I know. What if I style it for her with stuff she already owns?

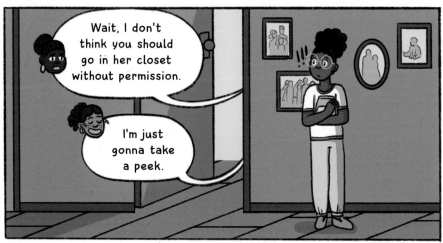

Wait, I don't think you should go in her closet without permission.

I'm just gonna take a peek.

Oh no. Do you want me to get your mom?

No, I just need to rest. Can you please go?

OK, we'll get out of your way.

Feel better, Charlie. Sorry about your closet.

I can't do this anymore.

CHAPTER
12

Charlie, it's time for school.

GROAN

PAT
PAT
PAT

TUG

UGH

You've been in bed all weekend.

What are you doing here?

Sorry to surprise you. How are you feeling?

Uh...still kind of sick.

That's too bad. Here, you dropped this.

Volume 4, huh? I just finished volume 3. You should let me borrow this when you're done.

You read comics?

Of course! I love comics. We should talk about them sometime.

That would be nice...

Well, I brought you your homework.

Oh, thanks.

But before I give it to you, can I ask you a question?

I guess?

It feels like you're always walking on eggshells around us. I just want you to act like yourself.

Easy for you to say. You already have friends, so you get to act however you want. Being the new girl is so much harder.

I know it seems that way, but it doesn't have to be hard. I know I can be bossy, and I say the wrong things sometimes, but my friends still like me for who I am.

I could try to be who I think people want me to be, but I wouldn't want to be liked for being someone I'm not. You shouldn't, either.

I just want a chance to get to know who you are. We all do.

If you let us. Here.

I hope you feel better soon, Charlie.

Also, we didn't want to do the presentation without you. Mr. Carter says we can wait until you're better, but right now we have an incomplete.

What? No way.

EW! HA HA HA HA HA HA HA

Yeah, I couldn't get the teacher's attention to ask to go to the bathroom, and I really had to go.

How did you live that down?

Some people made fun of me, but my real friends never did. I think that's when I learned who my real friends were.

Wow. That's way worse than having water spill on you.

Or there was the time I pretended to be good at guitar to impress a girl I liked who only dated guys in bands.

So do you want to tell me what happened that was so bad?

Well...it's never been easy for me to make friends.

I felt like if I could control how people saw me this time, I could guarantee they would like me, but I just ended up pushing them away.

I want people to know and like the real me. Pretending is hard, but I'm still afraid they won't like me once they actually get to know me.

I think I have an idea of how to show them who I am.

That's my girl.

CHAPTER 13

I was wrong about only getting one chance to start over.

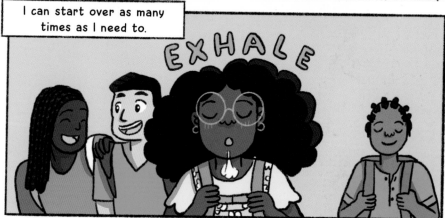

I can start over as many times as I need to.

Thanks, I'm fine. Sorry to make you worry.

I actually have something to confess.

SHUFFLE

What is it?

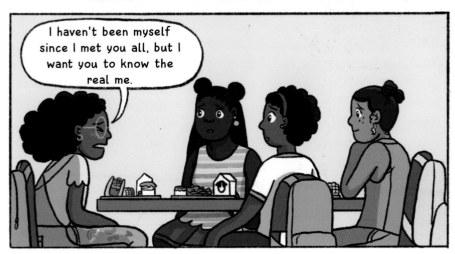

I haven't been myself since I met you all, but I want you to know the real me.

The truth is, I...I'm not fashionable at all. I was just copying magazine styles. Also, I read comics and watch cartoons, even though I'm probably too old for that now, and...I really hate the tapioca pearls in boba. Sorry I lied to you. Can we please still be friends?

Of course we're still friends. I'm sorry you felt like you needed to lie.

Yeah, we always just wanted to get to know you.

If you could be anyone in the world, who would you be? An athlete? A nerd? The most popular girl in school? How about yourself?

It may be scary at first, but once you let your guard down and be true to yourself, you'll find people who accept you for who you are.

That's how you find your true friends.

ACKNOWLEDGMENTS

The first book in the Curlfriends series celebrates friendship, being yourself, and father-daughter relationships. I lost my father while I was working on this book, so the moments Charlie was able to have with her dad were bittersweet for me. I put so much of my father into Charlie's dad. He was in the air force, goofy, outgoing, and affectionate. I couldn't have such a sweet and open heart-to-heart with him in real life, but I am happy I could have that moment through Charlie. I also lost my sister, who was a huge influence for me becoming an artist. This was sudden and unexpected, but I also wanted to honor her. I was happy I could represent her as Ms. Adrienne, Charlie's quirky and passionate art teacher. I hope knowing the meaning behind these characters and their relationships helps you enjoy their story even more.

This book was a labor of love that I couldn't have done without all the support I received from my family and my publishing team. I want to thank my editors, Andrea and Nikki, for helping me tell this story and sticking with me through these tough times. Thank you to my agent, Monica, for always seeing the value in my work and encouraging me along the way. Thank you to my spouse and son for putting up with my long nights and weekends drawing away. Thank you to my friends who inspired my story and my mom for always believing in me.

Until next time. Happy reading!

SHAREE MILLER is the author and illustrator of *Princess Hair*, *Don't Touch My Hair!*, and *Michelle's Garden*. She is also the illustrator of the Shai & Emmie series written by Quvenzhané Wallis and Nancy Ohlin and *The Excursion* written by Lauren Telesz and published in partnership with the Make-A-Wish® program. She lives in Jersey City with her spouse, son, and two cats, Pumpkin and Spice! Sharee invites you to visit her at shareemiller.com.